9/01

D.W.'s Library Card

Marc Brown

 Little, Brown and Company
Boston   New York   London

For Jo Ann Mitchell,
a very special librarian

First Edition

Based on a teleplay by Peter Hirsch

D.W.™ is a trademark of Marc Brown.

Library of Congress Cataloging-in-Publication Data

Brown, Marc.
  D.W.'s library card / Marc Brown. — 1st ed.
    p. cm.
  Summary: After finally getting her first library card, Arthur's little sister, D.W., tries to check out her favorite book with humorous results.
  ISBN 0-316-11013-2
  [1. Libraries — Fiction. 2. Books and reading — Fiction. 3. Brothers and sisters — Fiction. 4. Aardvarks — Fiction.] I. Title.
PZ7.B81618 Dyr 2001
[E] — dc21   00-042805

10 9 8 7 6 5 4 3 2 1

WOR

Printed in the United States of America

On Saturday, Arthur and D.W. went to the library.
"Will you check this book out for me?" asked D.W.
"I can't check out baby books," Arthur said. "It could go on my record!"
"When I have my own library card," said D.W., "I'll check out whatever I want!"

"When can I get a library card?" D.W. asked Ms. Turner.
"As soon as you can write your full name," Ms. Turner
said.
"But I hardly ever *say* my full name!" said D.W. "How
can I *write* it?"

"*I* can write *my* full name," bragged Tommy Tibble.
"Me, too," said Timmy Tibble.

At home, D.W. practiced writing her full name.

Arthur came in to see how she was doing.
"Doba Minifred Reabed? Who's that?" he asked.

At dinner, D.W. asked Mother and Father, "Why didn't you name me something easy, like 'A'?"
Mother looked at D.W.'s plate. "Well, you're almost there," she said.

D.W. gasped. "Quick, more mashed potatoes!"
After Father gave her another scoop, D.W. wrote "Read."
"I wrote my name! I wrote my name!" D.W. shouted.

On Saturday, D.W. was ready to get her library card.
"Very nice, Dora Winifred Read," said Ms. Turner.
"Here's your card."
"Hurray!" said D.W. "Now I can check out any book
I want!"
She went to find the frog book. But it wasn't there.

"That book was just checked out," said Ms. Turner. "It should be back in a week."

"A whole week?" D.W. said.

"Well, it might be back before then," Ms. Turner said.

All week, D.W. checked to see if the book had been returned.

The next Saturday, D.W. was the first one at the library, but the frog book still wasn't there. She waited and waited and waited.

"Hi, D.W.!" said a voice.

It was Tommy Tibble, and his brother Timmy was holding the frog book!

"You two had it!" said D.W. "And you hurt it! It's all wrinkly!"

"It was like that when they checked it out," Ms. Turner said. "It's an old book."

"We would never hurt a library book!" said Timmy.

"If you do," Tommy whispered, "they take away your library card *forever!*"

Ms. Turner checked the book out on D.W.'s card.
"Here you go," she said, handing it to D.W. "Take good care of it."
"Or else!" whispered Timmy.

On Saturday, D.W. carefully brought the book downstairs.

"Time to return this!" she said. "Finally!"

"Why are you wearing oven mitts?" asked Arthur.

"To keep it safe," said D.W.

At home, D.W. put the book in a safe place.
Every day, she checked to make sure it was all right.

The book looked so old.
D.W. imagined what would happen if she ruined it.
She would never be able to check out books again!

"It won't explode," said Arthur. "Did you like it?"
"I didn't open it," said D.W. "The Tibbles said the library would take my card away if I hurt the book. It's old! It could fall apart any minute!"
"Well," said Arthur, "if you're so worried, *I'll* open it. Hey, my name's in here! I checked this book out, too!"
"You checked out a baby book?" said D.W.
"It's not a baby book! It's a great book for little kids."
Arthur began to read.

When Arthur finished reading, D.W. sniffled sadly.
"It was a happy story," said Arthur. "Didn't you like it?"
"I loved it," said D.W. "I'm sad that I have to return it!"
"But you can check it out again," Arthur said.
"I can?" said D.W.
"It's called 'renewing,'" explained Arthur.

"Hurray!" D.W. said. "Then you can read it to me every day! Twice a day! Once in the morning and once at night! Then I can renew it again, and again, and again...."